◄ NATIVE AMERICAN PEOPLE ►

THE
COMANCHE

by Sally Lodge

Illustrated by Katherine Ace

ROURKE PUBLICATIONS, INC.

VERO BEACH, FLORIDA 32964

CONTENTS

© 1992 by Rourke Publications, Inc.

Printed in the USA

Library of Congress Cataloging-in-Publication Data

Lodge, Sally, 1953-
   The Comanche / by Sally Lodge.
     p.   cm. —(Native American people)
   Includes index.
   Summary: Examines the history, traditional lifestyle, and current situation of the Comanche Indians.
     1. Comanche Indians—Juvenile literature. [1. Comanche Indians. 2. Indians of North America.] I. Title. II. Series.
   E99.C85L63 1992   973'.04974—dc20   91-4114
   ISBN 0-86625-390-4   CIP
                                                                          AC

INTRODUCTION

Centuries ago, the Comanche—who eventually became famous horsemen of the Southern Plains—lived in the northern mountains of Wyoming and Montana. At that time, they were part of the Shoshone tribe, sometimes called the Snake People. For many generations after the two groups split, members of other Native American tribes would refer to the Comanche in sign language by drawing a snake-like figure in the air.

The members of the Shoshone tribe who would become the Comanche first began their migration southward at the end of the 1600s, when the Shoshone nation split into two bands. One group remained in the north, and the other moved into the area that is now Colorado. Hunting buffalo as they moved into the Southern Plains, this second group met up with a tribe called the Ute, which had also migrated from the mountains in the north.

It was the Ute who gave these southern Shoshone the name by which they came to be known. Traveling together into New Mexico in the early years of the 18th century, the two tribes encountered Spanish settlers. The Ute, who had been trading with the Spanish for years, introduced their Shoshone companions as *Koh-Mahts*, meaning "stranger." The Spanish interpreted this word as *Komantcia*, which evolved into *Comanche*.

The Comanche spent the first half of the 18th century establishing themselves as rulers of the Southern Plains. The area's mild climate and abundance of buffalo made it a highly desirable place to live. After driving the Apache out of the region, the Comanche took over a huge expanse of land that covered the southeastern corner of Colorado, southwestern Kansas, eastern New Mexico, and the central and western sections of both Oklahoma and Texas. This area, which became known as the *Comancheria*, remained under the tribe's control until 1875.

Throughout years of trading with the French and Spanish, and during their later association with the Mexicans, Texans and settlers from the East, the Comanche were fiercely protective of their territory. Yet as the 19th century wore on, it became clear that this proud tribe's years of rule over the Southern Plains were drawing to a close. As the white man's frontier advanced farther and farther west, the Comanche could no longer keep cattlemen and homesteaders off the Comancheria. But these mighty horsemen did not give up their cherished lands without a determined fight.

the COMANCHE

Masters of the Horse

HORSES were first introduced to the New World in 1519, when Spanish explorers brought them to Peru. By the end of the 16th century, the Spanish had moved north from Mexico, and had established settlements along the Rio Grande River. The Spanish tried hard to keep their precious horses out of the hands of the Pueblo and other tribes in the Southwest, but to no avail. The nomadic buffalo hunters of the Southern Plains realized how valuable horses were, and went to great lengths to obtain them.

A Comanche legend describes how the tribe acquired its first horses. According to this tale, a group of Spaniards appeared one day at a Comanche camp, riding what the Comanche described as "magic dogs." The Spanish camped with the Comanche for several days. When they took their leave and headed west, a group of Comanche followed them, hoping to find an opportunity to steal some of their enticing magical creatures.

For many nights the Spanish kept guard over the horses; the Comanche could not get close to them. One day the Spanish entered a walled town and left the horses unattended outside. The Comanche then quietly led the horses away, and took them back to their camp. In no time at all, the tribe learned to ride these "magic dogs" bareback, and discovered just how valuable they were.

Whether this tale is fact or folklore, it is true that the Comanche came to be known for their frequent, successful raidings of the horse herds owned by other tribes, as well as horses owned by the Spanish living in New Mexico, Texas, and northern Mexico. Sometimes the Comanche staged attacks on large settle-ments, openly seizing large herds belonging to the residents. Other times, they were much more subtle, sneaking into camps and stealing horses from beneath the noses of their sleeping owners.

The Comanche became legendary for their riding skills. At an early age, Comanche boys learned to ride horses, and spent much of their time racing each other on horseback. Although the Comanche were unusually short-legged and not very graceful when on the ground, on horseback they were poised and statuesque.

Their superior horsemanship gave the tribe an important advantage in battle. Comanche warriors repeatedly astound-ed their enemies with one maneuver that was especially tricky. Riding on horses, they swung themselves under their horses' bellies. From this position, the warriors could aim and fire so that the enemy could not tell where the arrows were coming from. This was but one of many ways that the Comanches' skills on horseback served them well during their reign over the Southern Plains.

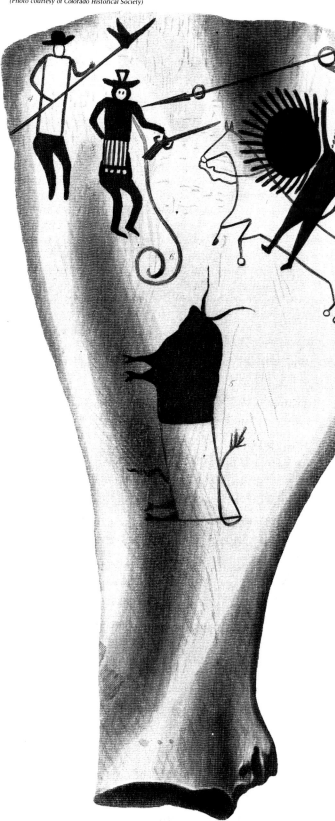

Comanche inscription on the shoulder blade of a buffalo.

The Comanche as Hunters

The acquisition of horses not only improved the Comanches' prowess as warriors, but also increased their efficiency in hunting buffalo and other game. On horseback, the Comanche and other Plains tribesmen could travel faster than the buffalo, and could follow the best herds wherever they went. The mounted hunters were able to surround and capture their prey much more easily than they had been able to do on foot.

The Comanche were known for their skilled marksmanship with bows and arrows, which they painstakingly crafted from various kinds of woods found on the Southern Plains. Even after other tribes had begun to rely on guns acquired from European traders, the Comanche continued to hunt buffalo

Comanches lived in tipis. A fire was built in the center and smoke escaped through the hole at the top. Meat is drying on the long pole.

and other game with their handmade bows and arrows.

Because buffalo herds were so plentiful on the Comancheria, the tribesmen hunted all year round. Since there were more than enough buffalo to go around, leaders of Comanche hunting expeditions did not impose restrictions on the tribesmen's hunting strategies. In this way, Comanche hunting methods differed from those of many Plains tribes, who often enlisted hunters to act as policemen. These guards observed the actions of the hunting party to make sure that the kill was distributed fairly. With the plentiful buffalo herds of the Southern Plains, Comanche hunters were given free reign to kill their prey.

The tribe also used horses to pull the *travois* (trav-WAH), primitive wagons fashioned from poles. Before that, dogs had been given this job. With the stronger horse performing the task, heavier loads of buffalo meat and hides could be pulled back to the Comanche camps.

The men and women of the tribe used virtually every part of the buffalo. Some of the meat was eaten fresh, and some was dried in the sun. A food staple of the Plains tribes was *pemmican*, which was made by pounding the dried meat into a powder and mixing it with melted fat and berries.

Tools made from buffalo horns were used in the cleaning and tanning, or softening, of the animal hides. After the hides were dried in the sun, they were made into clothing and covers for *tipis* (tee-PEES), funnel-shaped structures in which the Comanche lived. These resourceful Native Americans wasted no part of the buffalo. Muscle or sinew was used for thread and bowstring. Buffalo hair became brushes and rope, and household utensils were fashioned from the horns.

George Catlin painting of a Comanche village. Women are dressing robes and drying meat.

Tribal Structure

When the Comanche migrated to the Southern Plains, they retained some of the characteristics of the lifestyle they had known when they lived as Shoshone in the northern mountains. One thing that did not change was the tribal structure, which was very loosely organized. All Comanche members belonged to family hunting bands, which varied in size. The Comanche were not required to remain in a band with their blood relatives, but could leave one band and join another—or could even launch a new band. The size and strength of a band was always changing.

Over time, five main divisions of Comanche bands emerged. Each group became identified with the area of the Comancheria in which its bands lived and hunted. The largest and southernmost division was the *Penateka*. The *Nokoni*, who were the most nomadic Comanche people, remained mostly in the eastern section of the tribe's territory. North of them lived the *Kotsoteka*, who in

Too-hot-ko, son of Horseback, with feather bonnet, breastplate, bow and arrows.

turn were bordered on the north by the *Yamparika*, the last group to separate from the Shoshone. The final major division to form, the *Quahadi*, took up residence in the western stretches of the Comancheria, near the New Mexico-Texas border.

No central Comanche government ruled over these divisions. The groups shared a common language and culture, but functioned entirely independently of one another. Each band had its own political structure, the nucleus of which was the band council. All the adult male members of the band belonged to the council, which made important decisions for the band. Decision-making was often a lengthy ordeal for the Comanche bands, since the tribe members believed that all decisions should be unanimous. If a tribesman could not agree with a council ruling, he was expected to leave the band.

Each band had a principal band chief, and often a band was identified by his name. In addition to this leader, every band also had a war chief and a peace chief, both of whom had limited powers.

The war chief was usually appointed by the band council. For this honored position, the council selected a tribesman who had distinguished himself as a brave warrior. During a raid, the war chief had authority over all members of the war party. Once the raid ended, however, so did the war chief's term of command. Given the loose structure of the Comanche bands, it was not unusual for a warrior to decide to lead his own raid, and declare himself war chief of that expedition. If the warrior had a reputation for bravery and success in battle, others were likely to follow him.

Finally, each band had a peace chief, generally one of the respected elder males of the group. Often the role of peace chief was passed down from father to son. The peace chief acted as advisor and mediator to the band members. When it was necessary to make a critical decision about the band's internal affairs, the principal chief often consulted with the peace chief. But the Comanche's relaxed attitude toward political structure is also evident in the fact that a peace chief's period of leadership could end if the band members chose to ignore his suggestions.

Life in Comanche Society

Unlike many Native American tribes that inhabited the Plains, the Comanche did not establish permanent settlements and plant crops. Instead, they remained a hunting society, always traveling in pursuit of the finest buffalo herds. They lived on meat from the buffalo, deer, elk, and other game, as well as edible roots and the fruit of the persimmon, walnut, and elm trees that flourished on the Comancheria.

The nomadic life of the Comanche made the tipi an ideal structure to shelter the tribe members. Made from buffalo skins that the Comanche women carefully stitched together, these tipis could be taken down, rolled up for traveling, and reassembled in a very short amount of time. As in other Plains tribes, the women had the responsibility for packing up the family tipis each time the band moved from one camp to another.

Because the tribe was constantly on the move, the interior furnishings of the Comanche tipis were less elaborate than those found in the tipis of some tribes. The bed belonging to the head of the family was the main piece of furniture. It was made from piling buffalo-skin robes on top of each other. The remaining members of the family slept on similar, but smaller, piles of robes arranged around the main bed. The interior of the tipi was kept very neat. Food, clothes, and other belongings were stored in *parfleches* (PAR-flesh), strong pouches made of buffalo hide.

Buffalo hides, as well as deerskin, were also used by the women to make clothing for themselves and their families. In

warm weather, Comanche boys wore no clothing for almost the first decade of their lives. At that point, they began wearing breechclouts, or breechcloths, the traditional dress of Comanche men.

A breechclout was made from an ample piece of deerskin that stretched between the legs and was fastened to a leather belt in the back and the front. During mild seasons, Comanche men rarely wore clothing on the upper part of their body. When the chilly winter winds blew across the Southern Plains, they put on robes and high boots made from buffalo hides.

It was not considered proper for a Comanche girl to go without clothing, even in her early years. As a young girl, she wore a breechclout; when she reached adolescence, she adopted the clothes of Comanche women. The women wore loosely fitting, long-sleeved dresses, which they stitched together from pieces of deerskin and embellished with fringe, beads, and small pieces of metal.

Comanche men and women alike were fond of painting their bodies, faces, and scalps with brightly colored paints made from clay and from the juices of berries and other fruit. Men usually had pierced ears and hung several earrings from each earlobe. It was Comanche men rather than women who wore their hair long, separated into two braids that they then decorated with strips of fur, leather, and a single feather. Although girls often wore their hair in braids, Comanche women cut their hair much shorter than the men of the tribe.

Because of its decentralized organization, the Comanche tribe did not have some of the institutions that were important to other native nations of the Plains. Although warriors played a critical, highly-respected role in Comanche life, the tribe was not organized into military societies. Each band fought its own battles, sometimes with the help of neighboring bands. Every band bestowed its own military honors, or *coups* (KOO), on its war heroes. By Comanche standards, striking an enemy at close range—or even getting close enough to touch him—was considered an act of bravery worthy of reward.

The Comanche were also rare among the Plains tribes in that they did not have an annual tribe-wide assembly. Most other Plains tribes gathered together in the summer to hunt or perform religious ceremonies. One such important ritual was the Sun Dance, which the Plains tribes believed would regenerate the Earth and help them overcome their enemies in battle. Even though they were self-reliant and distinct from other Plains nations, the Comanche bands coexisted peaceably with them and prospered on the fertile Comancheria throughout the 1700s and the first half of the 19th century.

Making Friends and Enemies

The Comanche did not gain—nor maintain—control of their vast lands without a struggle. Although they succeeded in driving out the Apache, who had formerly occupied a large area of the Comancheria, the Apache remained a constant threat to the Comanche bands. For most of the 18th century, Comanche warriors staged raids on Apache settlements on the western and southern outskirts of Comanche territory.

The Comanche also clashed with other tribes, notably the Pawnee, the Osage, and the Arapaho. They had early skirmishes with the Kiowa, but this tribe eventually became strong and valuable allies of the Comanche. In addition to battling other tribes, the Comanche staged frequent raids on the Spanish settlements to their south and west.

Keeping these peoples off the land that the Comanche had claimed as their own—and away from the buffalo they considered theirs—was one of the key reasons the Comanche staged military offensives. But there was also another strong motivation for the frequent Comanche raidings: the tribesmen's burning desire to obtain additional horses and captives.

Captured men were either killed, traded as slaves to other tribes or to white traders, or ransomed at large trading fairs that were held in New Mexico.

Women and children were often taken as prisoners and brought back to Comanche camps. Here they performed many of the tasks expected of Comanche women and children, and were eventually assimilated, or absorbed, into the tribe.

The horses and captives seized by the Comanche during these raids helped the Comanche forge a bond with a group of white men that appeared on the Southern Plains during the 1720s: the French traders. In exchange for horses, mules, and captives—as well as buffalo hides and pelts from other animals—the French gave the Comanche and members of other tribes such valuable goods as guns, ammunition, knives, metal tools, and textiles. These traders and the Comanche established a friendly, mutually beneficial relationship.

As the Comanche realized the value of these newly acquired items, their demand for horses, captives, and buffalo only grew. Competition to secure these goods to trade greatly increased warfare and enmity among the Native Americans of the Plains.

The trade with the French also encouraged the Comanche to step up their widespread raidings of Spanish settlements. Searching for fresh herds of Spanish horses and captives, the Comanche rode farther and farther south, raiding Spanish and Pueblo Indian settlements in Mexico as well as Texas.

Although many bands of Comanche established a friendly trading relationship with the Spanish in New Mexico, the hostilities between the tribe and the Spanish in the more southern locations had reached a new—and decidedly dangerous—peak by the last decades of the 18th century.

A Fragile Peace with the Spanish

The number of French traders on the Plains declined sharply after 1763, when the British triumphed over the French in the French and Indian War. With the threat of French interference gone, the Spanish government sent several officials to the New World in hopes of establishing control over this area and restraining the hostile Native American tribes.

One of these men, Don Juan Bautista De Anza, was determined to halt Comanche raids on Spanish camps. With the help of Ute and Apache warriors, his troops entered Comanche territory in the summer of 1779 and staged an attack on a group of tribesmen. Green Horn, a well-respected Comanche war chief, was killed in the assault.

In 1786, hoping to prevent further invasions and to improve their deteriorating trading relationship with the Spanish, separate bands of Comanche traveled into New Mexico and Texas for peace talks. At De Anza's insistence, the Comanche bands agreed to let a single leader—Leather Jacket—represent the tribe in the negotiations. The two sides reached an agreement: The Comanche were to cease their raids on the Spanish who, in turn, would reestablish trade with the tribe.

The pact also allied the Spanish and Comanche against the Apache and the Pawnee, two long-time Comanche foes. In the 1790s, however, the Spanish played a peacemaking role when they helped to secure a truce between the Comanche and two tribes living north of the Comancheria: the Kiowa and the Kiowa-Apache. These nations were to become close friends of the Comanche.

For 50 years, this treaty kept peace between the Spanish of New Mexico and the Comanche bands living in the western sections of the Comancheria. Unfortunately, because of the lack of tribal unity, the Comanche bands in the south did not believe that the truce applied to them. They continued to invade the camps of the Spanish in Texas, looting their herds of horses and cattle.

Ironically, these Comanche would then take their bounty into the territory of the Spanish in New Mexico, where they would trade it for weapons and other manufactured goods. At best, the Treaty of 1786 brought only a fragile peace.

The Comancheria Is Invaded

The opening years of the 19th century brought significant changes—and an enormous number of outsiders—into the territory that the Comanche guarded so vigilantly. In 1803, the United States under President Thomas Jefferson purchased the Louisiana Territory from France. This important acquisition doubled the size of the country, and opened up its western expanses to adventurous settlers and traders. For the most part, the first easterners who traveled westward into Texas settled in the area east of the Comancheria, and were ignored by the Comanche.

The U.S. government was intent on moving another sizable group of people—eastern Native Americans—out of the eastern sections of the country, in order to make room there for more white settlers. To achieve this goal, the government passed the Indian Removal Act in 1830.

This law forced thousands of members of eastern tribes to leave the areas they had long inhabited and move to a tract of land known as the Indian Territory, located just east of the Comancheria. The Comanche resented the presence of relocated tribes, who often trespassed on their turf to hunt buffalo. As a result, there were frequent skirmishes between the Comanche and these newcomers to the Southern Plains.

The government sent several delegations into the area to try to persuade the Comanche to make peace with the transplanted tribes. In 1835, a pact was finally made, and the Comanche agreed to share their hunting grounds with the easterners. The tribe also made peace and began trading with the Osage, who had fought the Comanche for generations.

Though the Comanche came to terms with this wave of newcomers, their arrival was the beginning of the westward expansion that eventually toppled Comanche reign over the Southern Plains.

George Catlin painting of a Comanche meeting with white representatives of the U.S. government.

(Photo courtesy of National Museum of American Art, Washington, D.C./Art Resource, NY)

(Photo courtesy of Western History Collections, University of Oklahoma Library)

The surrender of Santa Anna to General Sam Houston (lying against tree).
Photo of a painting by R.J. Oderdonk.

Trying Times in Texas

The last years of the 1830s and the first half of the next decade were troublesome times for the Comanche. More and more white settlers from the East were establishing homesteads in Texas. As they situated their farms closer and closer to the borders of the Comancheria, the Comanche felt increasingly threatened, and began attacking these settlements regularly.

The situation worsened after 1836, when Texas won its independence from Mexico. Free land was offered to Americans interested in moving to the new Republic of Texas. A new wave of settlers poured into the area to take advantage of this deal and establish farms. Unfortunately, some of the land they settled on belonged to the Comanche.

The leaders of the Republic did not recognize the tribe's claim to the portion of the Comancheria that was in Texas, and instead proclaimed that any area not held by white men was up for grabs. The Comanche responded to this invasion of their lands by staging continuous raids on the new settlements. The Republic struck back by sending the Texas Rangers, a forceful band of soldiers, into the Comancheria to subdue the angry Comanche tribesmen.

After the Rangers had killed many Comanche on their own land, tribe members decided to seek a truce. At the beginning of 1840, a group of Comanche, led by Muguara, a principal chief of one of the bands, traveled to San Antonio to meet with Texan officials.

The white men demanded that the Comanche return captives that Muguara insisted the tribe was not holding. An argument followed, and the Texans decided to take the Comanche representatives as hostages. When the tribesmen tried to flee, the Texans opened fire. Muguara and several dozen other tribesmen were killed, and the rest of the Comanche delegation were taken prisoner.

This incident, known as the Council House Massacre, launched a new series of Comanche attacks on white settlers, who were arriving in Texas in growing numbers. In return, the Texas Rangers made many incursions into the Comancheria, burning villages, slaying tribe members, and stealing or shooting vast herds of horses. The Comanche were never able to recover from the devastation left by these violent raids.

In 1844, Sam Houston, the President of Texas, signed a treaty with the Comanche, but neither side was able to abide by its terms. The differences between the two sides were irreconcilable: The Comanche wanted a guarantee that white settlers and travelers keep out of their territory. It was a pledge that the Texans were not able or willing to make.

When Texas joined the United States in 1845, any possibility of the Comanche request being honored vanished. Thousands of new American settlers streamed into the new state during the next few years. This influx of white homesteaders drove many members of other Native American tribes onto Comanche land, where competition for the shrinking buffalo herds became fiercer than ever.

As the first half of the 19th century came to a close, the situation of the proud Comanche tribe had gone from bad to worse.

Sam Houston.

The 1850s: A Decade of Unrest

The federal government was no more successful than the Texans had been in keeping peace with the Comanche. Pacts were broken—by both sides—before the ink on treaty papers had a chance to dry. Given the increasing flow of white settlers into the Southern Plains, there was much less of a chance to satisfy Comanche demands for keeping outsiders off the Comancheria.

Then in 1848, gold was discovered in California, inducing an unprecedented number of easterners to stream across Texas—and the Comancheria—in the years that followed. This onslaught of

prospectors further depleted the buffalo herds and caused widespread outbreaks of cholera, smallpox, and other diseases to which the Comanche had no resistance.

In the mid-1850s, U.S. government officials devised a plan meant to solve their problems with what they regarded as disgruntled, hostile tribes. Two small tracts of land in Texas were set aside as reservations where the Native Americans in the state were expected to live. With the help of agents sent by the Bureau of Indian Affairs, the Comanche and members of other tribes were supposed to learn to live according to white people's customs and rules. By forcing the tribes to abandon their land and their lifestyle, the government hoped that peace would

at last be established in Texas and the other western territories.

This early attempt to place the Plains tribes on reservations was largely a failure. Most of the Comanche refused to leave the Comancheria, though they lived there under increasingly grim conditions. Feeling threatened by an ever-growing number of strangers, tribesmen continued to assault settlers on the outskirts of Comanche land. And many Comanche bands were themselves under constant siege by both the Texas Rangers and U.S. troops.

With this turmoil—and with their horse and buffalo herds dwindling rapidly—the Comanche were a sadly weakened nation by the end of the 1850s.

The Treaty of Medicine Lodge Creek

Throughout the early 1860s, the Comanche and other tribes of the South and Central Plains continued to attack white travelers and settlers, as well as the workers who were trying to lay the tracks for the first cross-country railroad. Determined to put a stop to these raids, the federal government sent a peace commission to talk with representatives of a number of tribes.

In October 1867, close to 5,000 Comanche, Kiowa, Kiowa-Apache, Arapaho, and Cheyenne tribesmen traveled to Medicine Lodge Creek in Kansas to meet with the government officials. It was a most dramatic assembly: Thousands of Native Americans witnessed the proceedings on horseback, while their leaders sat on logs arranged in rows in front of the commissioners.

Government spokesmen, who always seemed to emphasize what the government wanted to give the tribes and to ignore what it planned to take away from them, made proposals that the Native Americans did not like. Government officials wanted to persuade the tribesmen to abandon their nomadic,

(Photo courtesy of Colorado Historical Society)

Comanche brave in traditional costume.

hunting lifestyle and, instead, to farm the land. The government hoped that, as farmers, the Comanche would stay put and be less interested in controlling vast areas of the Southern Plains for their hunting grounds. The peace commission promised to give the Native Americans farm land, equipment, and cattle.

As part of this strategy to convert the tribes to farming, the government was taking away something that was very important to the Native Americans. The treaty drastically reduced the expanse of territory that the various tribes were to control. The Comanche were stripped of all their land in Texas, and were relegated to a tract of land between the Washita and the Red Rivers in Oklahoma.

The proposal for the new reservation was not at all acceptable to the Comanche. At the council, Ten Bears, one of the tribe's leaders, spoke eloquently about the importance of the wide-open prairie lands to his people. Leaders from other tribes also voiced their objections to the reduction of their territories. As a result of this outcry, the government agreed to let the Comanche and the Kiowa hunt on the lands they previously held in southern Kansas and the Texas panhandle.

For a number of Comanche tribesmen, this was not enough. Many refused to leave the original Comancheria, and had no intention of moving to the newly formed reservation. Since some bands had sent no representatives to the council at Medicine Lodge Creek, they insisted that the treaty did not apply to them. Others believed that, since they had voiced such strong objections to certain terms of the treaty, they were not bound by the offensive provisions.

Although many Comanche and members of other tribes ignored some of its terms, the Treaty of Medicine Lodge Creek marked the end of the tribe's traditional lifestyle on the Southern Plains. Most significantly, the 1867 treaty formally established the reservation way of life for the Comanche.

The pact also called for a halt to all attacks on the workers laying the railroad tracks. By agreeing to this term, the Comanche and members of other tribes helped pave the way for further development of the western lands. The transcontinental railroad brought more white travelers and settlers than ever into the Southern Plains. The area no longer was the land where the buffalo roamed and the Comanche hunted so freely.

Two Comanche, in Sun Dance costume, perform before observers in a tent.

The Comancheria Crumbles

In the years following the signing of the Treaty of Medicine Lodge Creek, white people came in growing numbers to hunt buffalo on the former Comancheria, wiping out the once plentiful herds. Resigned to the fact that they could no longer survive as hunters, some Comanche bands went to live alongside the Kiowa and Kiowa-Apache on the land that the government had set aside for them. Life on the newly created reservation was hardly comfortable. The transplanted Native Americans discovered that the land was not well suited to farming, and the government failed to keep its promise to provide them with adequate food and other supplies.

Numerous bands of Comanche, choosing to cling to their hunting lifestyle, continued to search out buffalo and game to hunt. They fared no better than the tribe members on the reservation. There were so few buffalo left that these hunters were not able to feed their families. Some were even forced to eat their horses to avoid starving.

Desperate, many of these Comanche came to place their faith in Ishatai, a Comanche preacher who maintained that he had communicated with the Great Spirit. In 1874, under Ishatai's direction, the Comanche performed the Sun Dance, a religious ritual that the tribe had shunned up to that point. The ceremony was meant to gain the favor of the Great Spirit, who they hoped would help drive away the white people and restore the herds of buffalo to the Southern Plains.

In June of 1874, believing that this spiritual ceremony had given them special powers, Comanche warriors set out to do battle with the white interlopers. Joined by a group of Kiowa and Cheyenne tribesmen, they attacked a group of white hunters at Adobe Walls, a trading post in the Texas Panhandle. Although strong in number, the Native American forces were no match for the hunters, who were armed with powerful, accurate rifles and were protected by the post's strong walls. The Comanche quickly lost faith in the power of the Sun Dance, which they never again performed.

The number of government forts on the Southern Plains was growing, as was the number of federal soldiers stationed in the area. From Washington came the order to force the Native American resisters onto the reservations. From all directions, the Comanche were attacked by government troops, who destroyed many of the tribe's campsites and killed thousands of Comanche horses.

After the harsh winter of 1875, most of the Comanche remaining on the Plains gave up the fight and went to live on the reservation. No longer masters of the vast Comancheria, the tribe became resigned to a very different way of life. Although they had not relinquished their control willingly, the Comanche's 150-year domination of the Southern Plains was finally over.

George Catlin painting of a Comanche war party on the march.

Native girls playing on swings at Fort Sill Indian School.

Bleak Years on the Reservation

Life on the reservation was not easy for the Comanche. Most had no interest in farming, and longed to leave the reservation to hunt the remaining buffalo and other game. This was not allowed by government officials, who, in effect, made the Comanche prisoners on their own land.

Representatives from the Bureau of Indian Affairs were sent to the reservation with instructions to rid the tribe of their Native American lifestyle. The agents tried to persuade the Comanche to abandon their language and customs for those of white American society, but the schools the Bureau set up to teach Comanche children were poorly attended. The Comanche were not eager to change, and resented all attempts to assimilate them into the white people's world.

Those who reluctantly agreed to become farmers met with little success. Frustrated by the poor soil and excessively dry climate, many gave up trying to live off the land. Unable to hunt or to grow crops, the Comanche became entirely dependent on the government for food. The quality of the government rations was poor and the quantity insufficient. Many tribe members grew sick and even died. During their first decade on the reservation, many Comanche also died from frequent outbreaks of malaria, smallpox, and other diseases.

The Comanche and the Kiowa were also suffering at the hands of greedy Texans who crossed the border into the reservation to steal Comanche horses and other livestock. Since the agents refused to allow the residents of the reservation to leave, the tribe was not able to recover its stolen animals, nor could it initiate retaliatory action to discourage further thefts.

As a further affront, Texas cattlemen began trespassing on tribal lands as they drove their large herds to the cattle markets in Kansas. They also brazenly crossed over the border to use reservation land as grazing pastures for their animals. It appeared that the white people, who already controlled the rest of the country, even couldn't keep their hands off the extremely limited area that they had once yielded to the vanquished tribes.

The Leadership of Quanah Parker

Quanah Parker.

The last Comanche band to hold out against reservation life was led by Quanah (KWAH-nuh) Parker, who eventually surrendered to the U.S. Army in the late spring of 1875. Quanah had been a respected warrior during his band's days on the Southern Plains. After coming to live on the reservation, he rose to prominence as the principal chief of the Comanche, a position he held until his death in 1911.

The nature of reservation life changed the traditional political structure known to the Comanche. Government officials were not willing to recognize the authority of the leaders of the many individual bands. They preferred to talk to a single chief or spokesperson. Although Quanah spoke English poorly and relied on others to write his letters for him, he emerged as the individual that the government agents wanted to deal with.

Many white officials were intrigued with Quanah's mixed-blood heritage. His mother was Cynthia Anne Parker, a white woman who had been captured by the Comanche at the age of nine. Many years later, she was recaptured by whites and brought back to live in white society. Quanah's father was a Comanche war chief named Peta Nocona, who had been killed in a raid staged on a Comanche camp by frontiersmen.

Even-tempered, willing to listen, and ready to compromise, Quanah was an ideal liaison between government agents

Quanah Parker wearing a fringed buckskin shirt, leggings, and an eagle feather bonnet with full train.

Though his personal gains caused other Comanche to resent him, Quanah also negotiated effectively on behalf of the tribe. In 1884, he traveled to Washington with another Comanche chief and a cattleman. Their mission was to persuade government officials to approve a leasing arrangement whereby the ranchers would pay the tribe for use of certain pasture lands. Although the government officially refused to grant permission, Quanah was able to persuade the agent on the reservation to agree to the deal. As a result, the Comanche received a small but steady income—called a grass payment—from the Texans.

It did not take long for Quanah to establish his reputation as an amiable, intelligent leader. In government circles, he was praised for cooperating with officials and for doing his best to enforce the white people's policies among his tribe. At the same time, he made some 20 trips to Washington during his lifetime to plead the Comanche cause to government representatives. He also performed ceremonial functions. He was asked to take part in the inauguration of President Theodore Roosevelt. Quanah's was a life that some fellow Comanche scorned, and others envied.

Government agents held Quanah up as an example of what Native Americans could achieve if they tried. Here was a man who had acquired many of the worldly goods coveted by white people. In addition to accumulating a herd of several hundred cattle, Quanah cultivated more than 100 acres of land. While many of his tribe ignored the wooden frame houses built for them by the government, preferring to remain in their tipis, Quanah built himself an

and the Comanche people. He was trusted by both sides, and was clever enough to make agreements that not only benefited the tribe, but worked to his personal advantage as well.

Quanah was one of the first Comanche leaders to raise his voice against the Texas ranchers' use of reservation land for grazing. Quanah met with the cattlemen and managed to get himself placed on their payroll as keeper of the peace between the ranchers and the tribe. At the same time, Quanah received livestock from the cattlemen. This enabled him to increase the size of the herd he had been allotted by the government.

elegant house with a two-story porch and splendid white stars on the roof. Such a display was impressive by anyone's standards.

Quanah dutifully followed most of the government's directives, including sending his children to the government's white-style schools and encouraging other Comanche to do the same. Yet the renowned chief also clung to a number of tribal traditions. Although he traded his buffalo-skin robes and moccasins for the suits, shirts, and shoes of white Americans, Quanah refused to cut his hair. Instead, he wore it in two long braids—Comanche-style.

Quanah Parker and one of his favorite wives.

Ella Maseet and Mary Parker, dressed in buckskin.

Some aspects of his lifestyle, however, were considered totally unacceptable by the white people with whom Quanah had contact. A confirmed polygamist, the chief insisted on living with more than one wife at a time. It is believed that at one point Quanah had as many as seven wives.

Furthermore, Quanah was a strong proponent and follower of the peyote religion—peyotism—which was discouraged by the government. This religion entailed using peyote in religious rituals. Peyote is a narcotic drug produced by a cactus plant of the same name. The peyote religion provided the Comanche with some reassurance as they tried to adjust to reservation life, and government agents eventually came to accept it as part of the Comanche way of life.

25

The Devastating Allotment Act

In 1887, Congress passed the Allotment Act, a law that brought further misery to the Comanche and other Native American tribes. Convinced that the tribes living together on reservations would never really learn to live according to white people's traditions, the government decided that tribes should not own land communally. Altering the reservation structure was even more important to the lawmakers for another reason. It meant that huge tracts of land would be opened up to white settlers.

Once robbed of their beloved Comancheria, the Comanche were now to be stripped of much of their reservation lands. The Allotment Act decreed that parts of each reservation were to be divided into small farms. Tribe members would receive their own plots of land, and the government would buy up the remaining tracts of the reservation—for small amounts of money. This land could then be sold—at great profit—to white developers and settlers.

Like numerous other tribes, the Comanche did not like what they heard. They had been told that their reservation would belong to them forever, and they did not want to sell out to the whites. For most of the tribe, the idea of owning and farming their own small, individual pieces of property held little appeal. They were used to owning their lands communally, and resisted the proposed change.

The 1867 Treaty of Medicine Lodge Creek, which had put the reservation system in place, stated that land owned by the Comanche, the Kiowa, and the Kiowa-Apache could not be sold without

Three Comanche women and a baby taken prisoner by U.S. troops near Adobe Walls, TX, 1868.

the approval of three-fourths of the adult males in the three tribes.

The government set up the Jerome Commission to negotiate with the tribes and to persuade them to accept allotment. To sweeten the deal, the commission increased the amount of acreage each tribe member was to receive. In addition, the tribe was promised a sum of money from the sale of the remaining reservation land to settlers.

The members of the commission finally succeeded in persuading enough members of the three tribes to approve the agreement. Many tribesmen had been pressured into signing the act by government representatives who threatened to enforce the less generous terms of the Allotment Act if the tribes did not approve the Jerome Agreement. In addition, many of those signing the agreement could not read or speak English, and may not have known exactly what they were signing.

Although signed in 1892, the Jerome Agreement was not ratified by Congress until 1900. In spite of the delay, the years in between brought many land-greedy white settlers onto the reservations. Some were so anxious to possess the land that they did not even wait until the government had bought it from the tribes and was ready to resell it. Instead, many whites simply seized parcels of land that still belonged to the tribes.

A vocal opponent of allotment, Quanah Parker had worked hard to bargain on behalf of his tribe. He traveled to Washington to present the Comanche case, and succeeded in delaying the allotment process for several years. During that time, Quanah was able to get the Jerome Agreement amended so that the Comanche, the Kiowa, and the Kiowa-Apache received a sizable tract of land to be held communally. This land was then leased to the ranchers, and the grass payments collected from them provided income for the tribe. Unfortunately, the tribes would be forced to sell the land to the government in 1906, and the last of the tribal lands would disappear.

After the Jerome Agreement took effect at the turn of the century, Quanah's wealth and influence declined significantly. No longer could he carry on lucrative practices such as leasing large tribal pastures to Texas cattlemen, and keeping most of the profits for himself.

Although he still held the title of principal chief of the Comanche, Quanah was now under stricter government control than ever. His title was in name only. When he died in 1911, no one was appointed to succeed him. Quanah Parker, once a great warrior on the Southern Plains, was the last of the great Comanche chiefs.

Comanche tipis were easy to put up and take down, so campsites like this could be moved easily.

The Comanche in the Twentieth Century

Having selected their 160-acre home-steads, the members of the Comanche tribe settled into a life of hard work with few rewards. Because the land given to them was not fertile farmland, most of the tribe found it difficult to survive on their limited income.

In 1907, the territory occupied by the Comanche, the Kiowa, and the Kiowa-Apache became part of the new state of Oklahoma. Soon after, the federal government gave the state the task of overseeing the financial affairs of the Native Americans living within its borders. Guardians were appointed to manage the property owned by the Comanche tribe, but many of these white trustees were dishonest and cheated the Comanche out of much of their land.

The early 1930s were dismal years for the Comanche. A severe drought struck Oklahoma, worsening the sorry plight of the farmers. In addition, the already poor tribe members were feeling the crippling effects of the Great Depression, the national economic crisis of the '30s.

But help was on the way. President Franklin D. Roosevelt launched his New Deal programs, some of which brought many positive changes into the lives of Native Americans. Although the Indian Reorganization Act of 1934, which par-tially reversed the unpopular Allotment Act, did not apply to the tribes living in Oklahoma, the government passed the Oklahoma Indian Welfare Act the following year. As a result of this law, the Comanche and their neighboring tribes in the state received money from the government for health care and educational programs.

In addition, the spirit of the New Deal encouraged a more sympathetic attitude toward Native Americans. The govern-ment repealed laws that forced the tribe to conform to the religious and educa-tional practices of white people. Tribes were also allowed to set up their own political structures. Disbanded at the turn of the century, the Comanche, Kiowa, and Kiowa-Apache Business Council was reestablished in the mid-1930s. It was the official tribal government of these tribes for 30 years.

The beneficial effects of what became known as the Indian New Deal were largely reversed in the years following World War II (1939-45). After the war, the Bureau of Indian Affairs seemed to do an abrupt about-face by introducing its policy of termination. By the policy, the government discontinued many of the programs it had begun to help the tribes, and attempted to relocate to cities many Native Americans still living on reservations. Termination hurt the Comanche mainly by withdrawing funding for health care and education.

For a tribe that historically had so little central organization, the Comanche have done a remarkable job of banding together in this century. In 1966, the tribe wrote its own constitution and formed the Comanche Business Committee to manage its financial matters. A Tribal Council, consisting of all Comanche adults, was also founded.

Present-day Comanche, like members of other tribes, face much racial prejudice, unemployment, and poverty. Although many tribe members have moved to California, Texas, and other states in hopes of finding better job opportunities, most remain in Oklahoma. Interestingly, evidence of the traditional Comanche band structure still exists, as members of various bands have settled together in specific sections of the state.

True to their heritage as warriors, many Comanche enter military service today. Two groups of ex-military tribe members—the Comanche Indian Veterans Association and the Little Ponies—conduct powwows and work to keep tribal traditions intact. In fact, these organizations gather the Comanche together for tribal celebrations each year, something that their ancestors on the Comancheria were too loosely organized to be able to do.

Although some present-day Comanche belong to Christian churches, a good many still practice the peyotism embraced by Quanah Parker in the late 1800s. Since 1918, use of peyote in religious ceremonies has been legal in Oklahoma.

Like other Native American tribes today, the Comanche are caught between two worlds: They are trying to preserve their cultural identity, while keeping up with the hectic pace of 20th-century America. The Comanche's 150-year reign over the Southern Plains was followed by more than a century of suppression by a white society that had no understanding of the heritage of these proud natives. Yet the tribe has persevered, and has kept alive many of the rich traditions that form the heart of the Comanche people.

Important Dates in Comanche History

1519   Spanish explorers bring horses to the New World.

1600s   Toward the end of the century, the Comanche migrate from the northern mountains to the Southern Plains.

1700s   In the early years of the century, the Comanche acquire horses and soon became master horsemen.

1720s   French traders appear on the plains, bringing guns and other manufactured goods to the Comanche.

1725   By this date, the Comanche establish themselves on the Comancheria.

1779   Don Juan Bautista De Anza is the first Spanish leader to attack the Comanche in their own territory.

1786   In the Treaty of 1786, the Comanche promise to cease their raids on the Spanish, and trade between the two groups is reopened.

1803   The Louisiana Purchase opens up western territories to white settlers and traders.

1830   Congress passes the Indian Removal Act, forcing many eastern tribes to relocate to Indian Territory in the Southern Plains.

1836   Texas gains independence from Mexico, encouraging a new wave of settlers to the area.

1840   Chief Muguara and other Comanche are slain in the Council House Massacre. Comanche raids that follow are put down by the Texas Rangers.

1845   Texas enters the Union, and thousands of white homesteaders enter the state.

1867   The Treaty of Medicine Lodge Creek establishes a reservation for the Comanche in Oklahoma.

1874   Encouraged by performing the Sun Dance, the Comanche attack but are defeated by white hunters at Adobe Walls in Texas.

1875   The last Comanche bands report to the reservation, ending the tribe's rule over the Southern Plains.

1880s   Quanah Parker becomes principal chief of the Comanche and secures revenues by establishing grass leases with Texas ranchers.

1887   Congress passes the Allotment Act, stripping the Comanche and other tribes of their tribal lands.

1892   The Jerome Agreement, amending some of the terms of the Allotment Act in the tribes' favor, is signed by the Comanche, the Kiowa, and the Kiowa-Apache.

1911   Quanah Parker, the last great Comanche chief, dies.

1935   The Oklahoma Indian Welfare Act, part of President Roosevelt's New Deal, helps the impoverished Comanche.

1940s   The U.S. government begins introducing its policy of termination, ending many programs intended to help Native Americans.

1966   The Comanche write a tribal constitution and form a Tribal Council and the Comanche Business Committee.

INDEX